Brer Anancy
and
Brer Duck

A Duck's Dream

V. S. RUSSELL

Illustrations by
Jagath Kosmodara

Brer Anancy Press

Ordering Information:

Quantity sales. Special discounts are available on quantity purchases by corporations, associations, and others. For details, contact:

Brer Anancy Press

3968 Crenshaw Blvd.

Los Angeles, CA 90008

info@breranancy.com

www.BrerAnancy.com

Printed in the United States of America

THIS BOOK BELONGS TO

_____

1

Anancy is a Spider
Anancy is a Man
Anancy is West Indian
Anancy is African

— Andrew Salkey

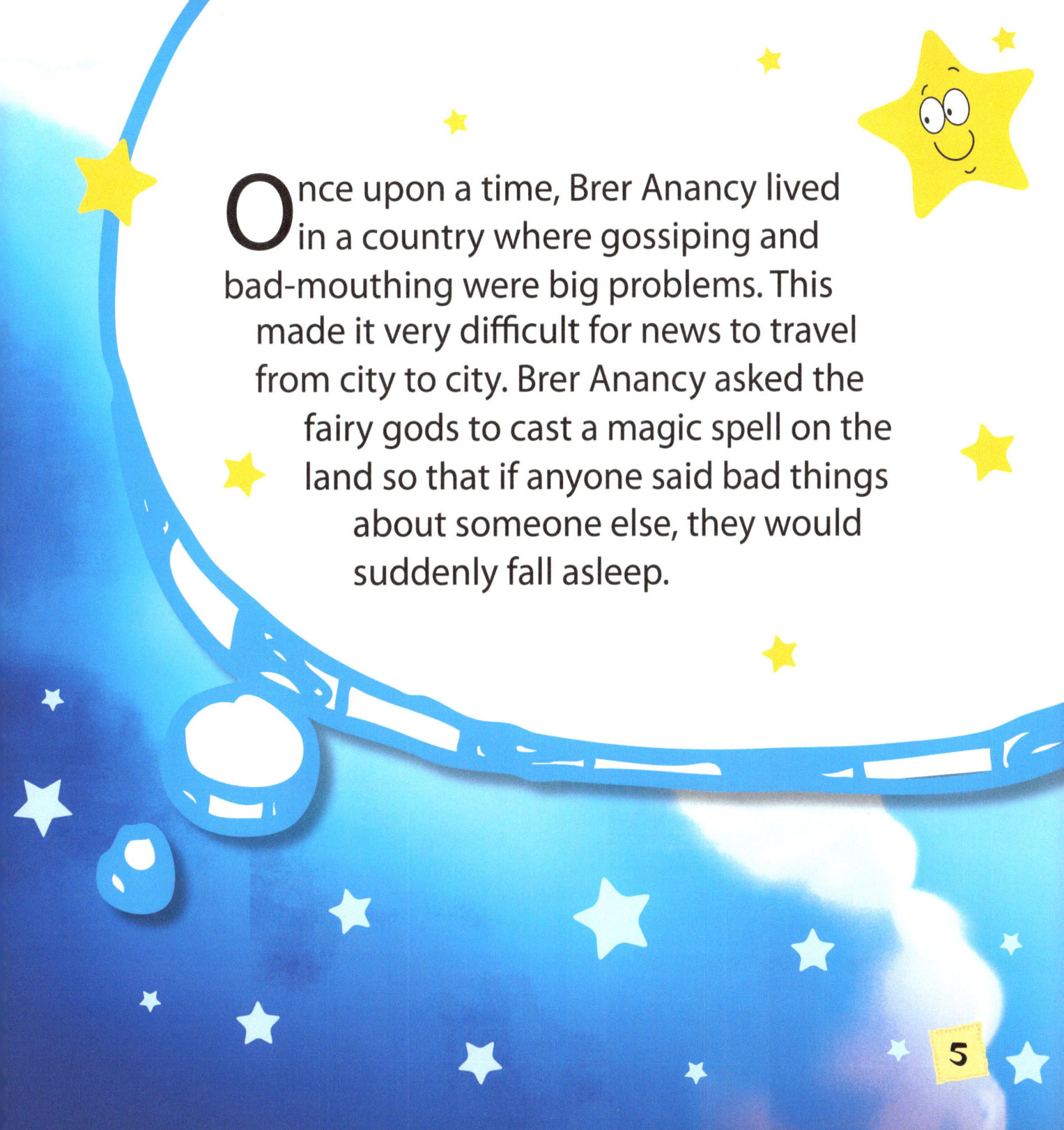

Once upon a time, Brer Anancy lived in a country where gossiping and bad-mouthing were big problems. This made it very difficult for news to travel from city to city. Brer Anancy asked the fairy gods to cast a magic spell on the land so that if anyone said bad things about someone else, they would suddenly fall asleep.

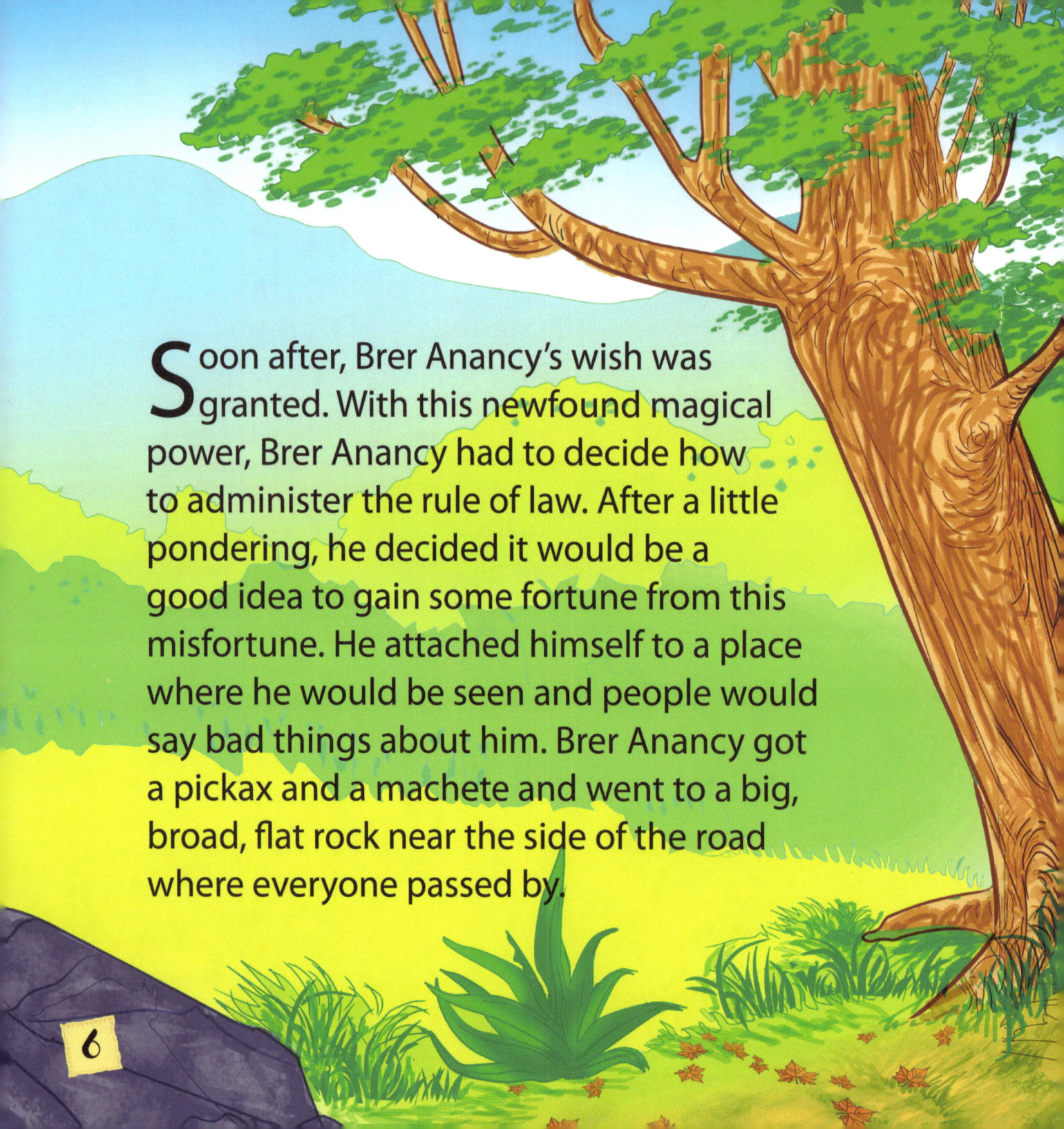

Soon after, Brer Anancy's wish was granted. With this newfound magical power, Brer Anancy had to decide how to administer the rule of law. After a little pondering, he decided it would be a good idea to gain some fortune from this misfortune. He attached himself to a place where he would be seen and people would say bad things about him. Brer Anancy got a pickax and a machete and went to a big, broad, flat rock near the side of the road where everyone passed by.

Brer Anancy began to knock: *Pong, pong, pong*. Brer Pig was passing by.

Brer Pig said, "Morning, Brer Anancy."

Brer Anancy said, "Morning, Brer Pig."

Brer Pig said, "What are you doing over there?"

8

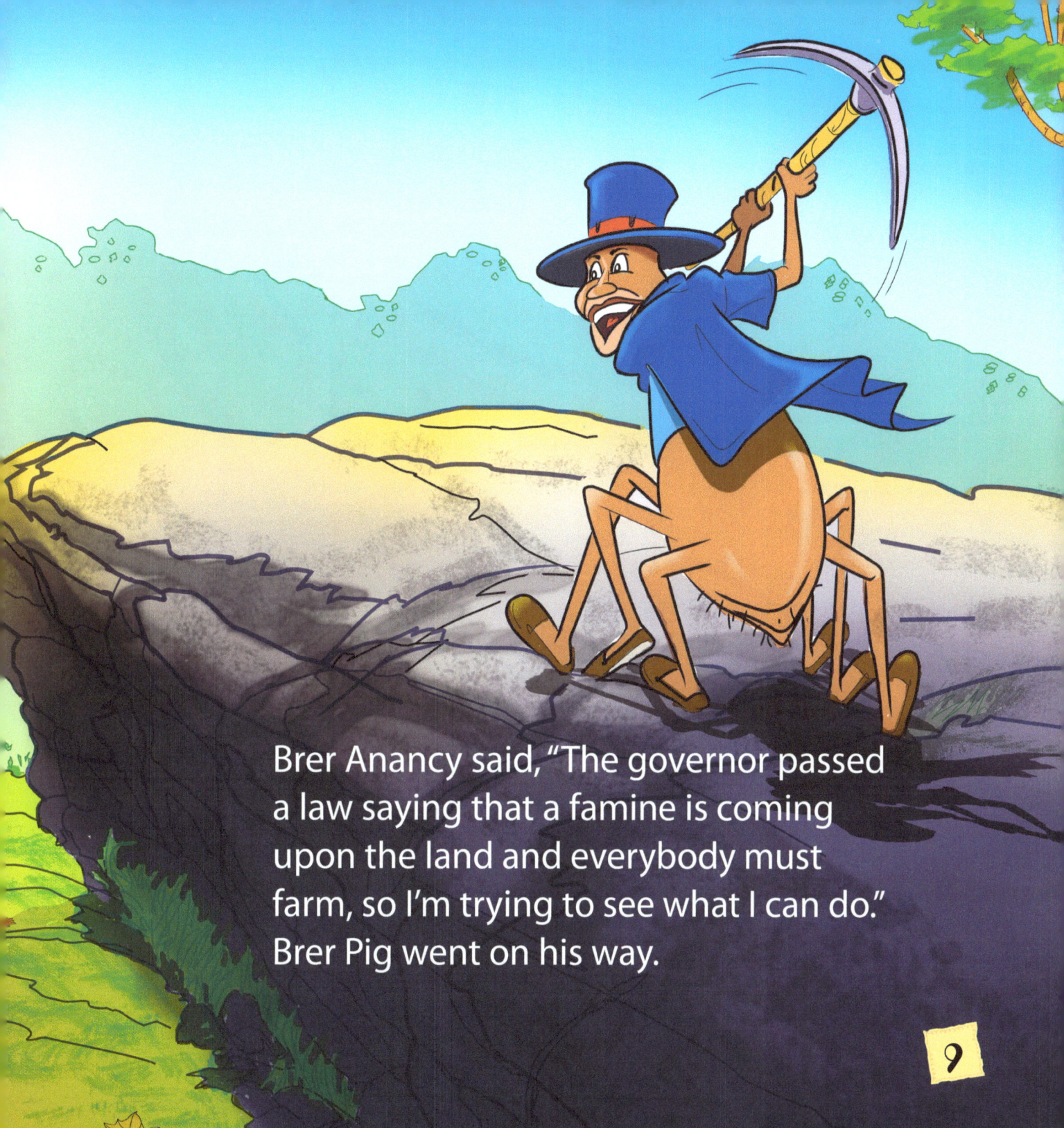

Brer Anancy said, "The governor passed a law saying that a famine is coming upon the land and everybody must farm, so I'm trying to see what I can do." Brer Pig went on his way.

9

After Brer Pig went a short distance, he said, "Other people farm on good soil, but Anancy is farming on rocky ground!" As Brer Pig uttered the last word, he suddenly fell to the ground and fell asleep.

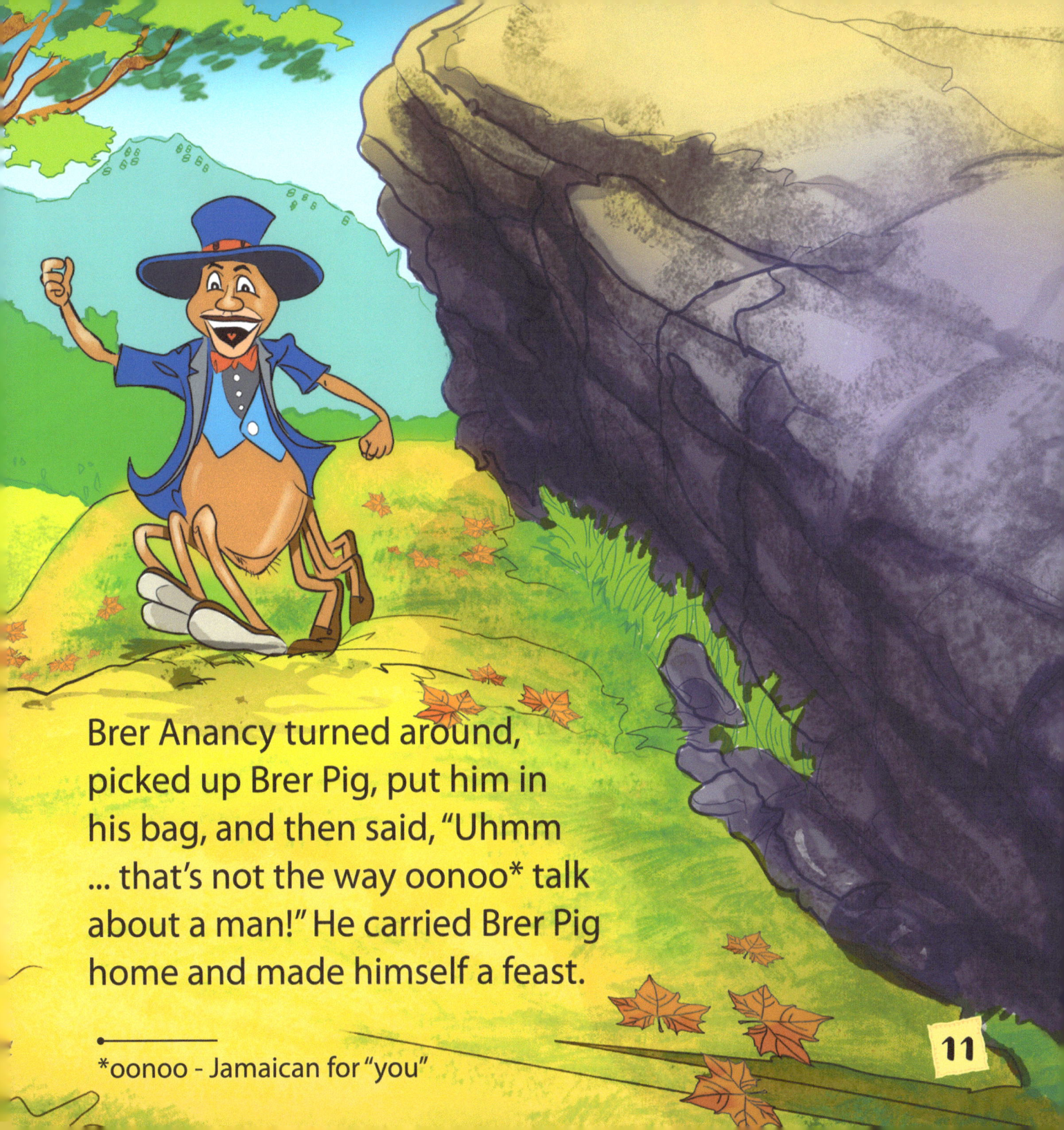

Brer Anancy turned around, picked up Brer Pig, put him in his bag, and then said, "Uhmm ... that's not the way oonoo* talk about a man!" He carried Brer Pig home and made himself a feast.

*oonoo - Jamaican for "you"

The next day, Brer Anancy went back to the same area. Brer Cow was passing by. Brer Anancy began to knock again: *Pong pong, pong.*

Brer Cow said, "Moo-orning, Brer Anancy."

Brer Anancy said, "Moo-ornin', Brer Cow."

Brer Cow said, "What are you doing over there?"

Brer Anancy said, "The governor passed a law saying that a great famine is coming upon the land and everybody must farm, so I'm trying to see what I can do."

Brer Cow went on his way.

As soon as Brer Cow got a distance away, he said to himself, "Other men farm on good soil, but Brer Anancy is farming on stones!"

Brer Cow suddenly fell to the ground and fell asleep.

Brer Anancy scampered over, picked up Brer Cow, put him in his bag, and said, "That's not the way oonoo talk about a man!"

He carried Brer Cow home and made himself another meal.

15

Brer Horse and Brer Goat came by, and they both shared the same fate.

18

A few days went by
while Brer Anancy
was there knocking, but
no animals passed by.

Suddenly one morning, Brer Duck came by. He said, "Morning, Brer Anancy."

Brer Anancy said, "Morning, Brer Duck."

Brer Duck said, "What are you doing over there?"

Brer Anancy said, "The governor passed a law saying that a great famine is coming upon the land and everybody must farm, so I'm trying to see what I can do."

Brer Duck said nothing.

Brer Anancy then said to Brer Duck, "What strange news comes from your neck of the woods?"

Brer Duck said, "Nothing strange, but I had a dream last night. In the dream, I was on earth too long and hadn't gotten married, so I have decided to go down to Ocho Rios to see if I can get wed." Then he went on his merry way.

Brer Anancy was amazed. He laughed and then said, "Good people get married. Long beak Brer Duck says he wants to get married, too!" Suddenly Brer Anancy fell asleep.

25

Brer Duck turned around, picked up Brer Anancy, put him in his bag, and said, "That's not the way oonoo talk about a man!"

A Anancy Mek It ... Jackmandora, mi no choose none!

27

Moral of the Story:
"If you don't have anything good to say, then say nothing bad!"

Glossary

Brer – Brother
Oonoo – Jamaican for "you"
Jackmandora – Keeper of heaven's door; doorman
A Anancy Mek It – It's of Anancy's making / It's an Anancy story
Mi No Choose None – I take no responsibility for the tale I have told

Brer Anancy
and
Friends

www.ingramcontent.com/pod-product-compliance
Lightning Source LLC
Chambersburg PA
CBHW040307250626

47171CB00009B/15